clouds

yogurt

P5

flowers

dress

birds

paper

paper

sky

keys

# the little word catcher

by Danielle Simard

illustrations by Geneviève Côté

Second Story Press

In memory of the years when I used to find the words for my mother.

*Danielle*

I should have liked to find those words – and some others – for Noëlla.

*Geneviève*

Did you know that words could get lost?
My grandmother misplaces her words all the time.
She loses them even more often than her keys.
Do they fly off just to play tricks on her?
I wonder where they go.

We always find
her keys somewhere.

But her words stay lost.
They aren't hiding in her purse
or at the bottom of the cupboard.

Since we really can't find them anywhere,
we decided to lend Grandma our words.

When Grandma says, "I can't find my... my... "
my mother and I ask, "Your keys?"
We're usually right, especially if she's
rummaging around in her purse.
But it's not always that easy.

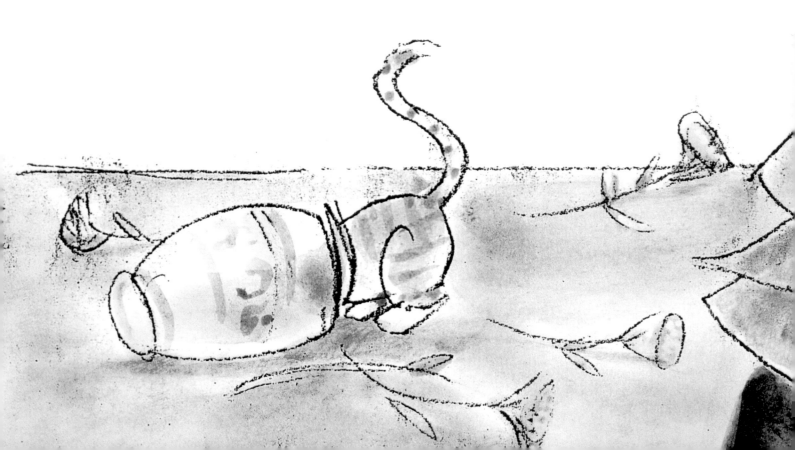

When we're at the supermarket
Grandma says,
"I must buy some... some..."
She looks like she's drying an invisible plate
because she's moving her hands
round and round.
"Do you want to buy dishwashing detergent?"
Mom asks her.

Grandma keeps on turning her hands in the air.
"I know!" Mom cries. "You want whipping cream!"
"No, not that!" Grandma is annoyed
because Mom got it wrong.
"You know what I mean. We use it every day!"
Mom looks away and sighs.
"No, I don't know, Mother."

My grandmother looks very sad.
Suddenly it seems like she's not with us.
And yet she is right there.
Mom just looks upset and
even sadder than Grandma.

I decide to find the lost word.
Let's see... what turns round and round?
Something we use every day...
"Toilet paper! Is that it?
You want toilet paper?"
"Yes. That's it, my sweetheart!"
Now Grandma is laughing.

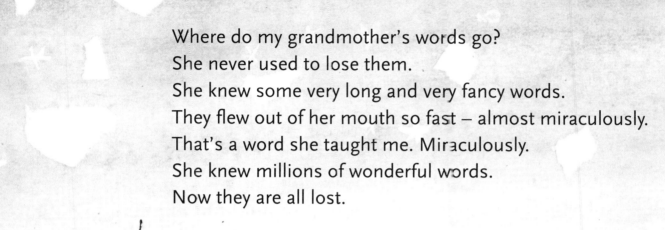

Where do my grandmother's words go?
She never used to lose them.
She knew some very long and very fancy words.
They flew out of her mouth so fast – almost miraculously.
That's a word she taught me. Miraculously.
She knew millions of wonderful words.
Now they are all lost.

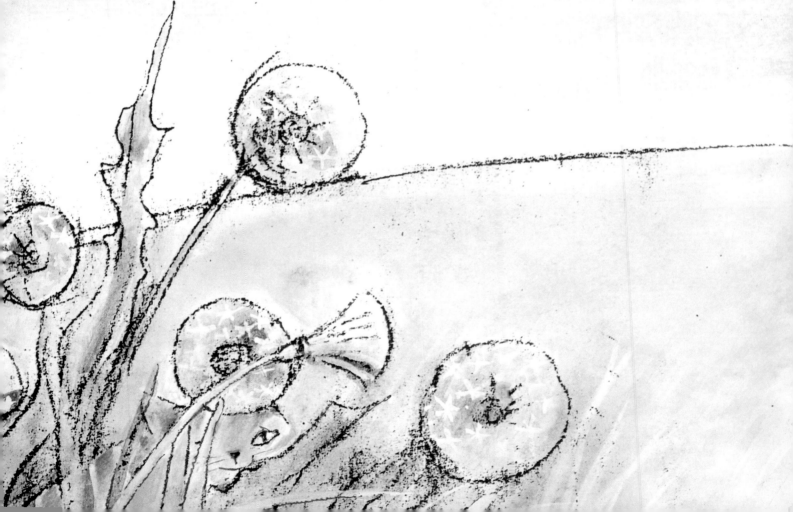

I want Grandma to be like she was when she remembered everything.
I guess I will have to find out where her words are hiding.
I could catch them all with a big net and bring them back to her.
Every single lost word. But I'd better do it quickly.
Because Grandma is losing more and more words all the time.

Now she's even forgetting my name.
She says to me, "Help me find my keys, Francine."
That's not me! My name's Elise. Her sister is called Francine.

I asked my dad why Grandma thinks I'm an old lady.
He said, "Grandma's sister, Francine, was once a pretty little girl who looked like you, Elise. She's mixing you two up."

It makes me feel strange to think about that.

Dad explained that everything gets old –
flowers, my cat, Fiddle,
even the living room furniture.

Well, maybe words get old too – like people.
Maybe the more we use them, the older they get.
Maybe Grandma has used her words
so much they're all worn out.

Like a dress you've had for years and years!

Dad says he doesn't believe it.
But I think that's Grandma's problem.
Her old words are wearing out, bit by bit.
And they leave her sentences full of holes.
"I've eaten the... the... You know, the..."
Grandma makes a shape with her fingers.
It looks like a little container.
"You've eaten all your yogurt?"
"Yes! Remind me to buy some when
we go... with your mother... You know,
down there..."
"To the supermarket?"

I feel like I'm playing a guessing game with Grandma.
It's a good thing I'm an excellent guesser.
Dad even calls me the little word catcher.
I don't really know why it is so easy for me.
Maybe I know the hiding places –
without even knowing that I know.
That must be it...
But when I bring the words back to Grandma,
she doesn't remember them for long.
How come?

What if my grandmother hasn't really lost her words?
What if she hasn't worn them out like her old dresses?
What if she is *giving* them to me instead?
That would explain it. Giving is giving.
Once you give something away, you can't take it back!

"Look, Francine, the pretty... that... that..."
"The pretty cloud that's blowing across the sky, Grandma?"
"That's right, my dear. It's like..."

Grandma lifts her arms up. She waves her hands in the air,
making a big flower opening its petals over our heads.
"Yes, Grandma, it's like the cloud is dissolving into the sky – miraculously."
"Miraculously? You know some amazing words sweetheart!"

Grandma isn't upset that she gave me her words.
And when I bring them back to her, she gives me a lovely smile.
Dad was wrong.
Some things never get old.
Grandma has been smiling that smile for a long, long time.
But it never wears out.

**Library and Archives Canada Cataloguing in Publication**

Simard, Danielle, 1952-
[Petite rapporteuse de mots. English]
The little word catcher / by Danielle Simard ;
illustrated by Geneviève Côté.

Translation of: La petite rapporteuse de mots.

ISBN 978-1-897187-44-9

I. Côté, Geneviève, 1964-  II. Title.

PS8587.I287P47313 2008      jC843'.54      C2008-902989-5

© 2007 Danielle Simard, Geneviève Côté
and les éditions Les 400 coups Montréal (Québec)
Translation by Jill Corner
Design by Mathilde Hébert and Melissa Kaita

Printed in China

*Second Story Press gratefully acknowledges the support of the Ontario Arts Council and the Canada Council for the Arts for our publishing program. We acknowledge the financial support of the Government of Canada through the Book Publishing Industry Development Program.*

  ONTARIO ARTS COUNCIL
CONSEIL DES ARTS DE L'ONTARIO

  Canada Council    Conseil des Arts
for the Arts      du Canada

Published by
Second Story Press
20 Maud Street, Suite 401
Toronto, Ontario, Canada
M5V 2M5
www.secondstorypress.ca

birds

sky

clouds

paper

yogurt

clouds

keys

flowers

paper